My G[...] Could do ANYTHING in SAN FRANCISCO

by Ric Dilz

To all the Grandmas who love their Grandchild
to the bay and back!

RICDesign LLC

Boulder, Colorado

Illustration & Design by: Nancy Maysmith, Helen H. Harrison & Ric Dilz

My Grandma could do ANYTHING...

My Grandma
doesn't bungee jump
from the
Golden Gate Bridge...

But she could!

My Grandma
doesn't
conduct a cable car...

But she could!

My Grandma
doesn't skateboard
down the world's
crookedest road...

But she could!

My Grandma
doesn't work in a
chocolate factory...

But she could!

My Grandma
doesn't play with seals
on Pier 39...

But she could!

My Grandma
doesn't climb up the side
of Coit Tower...

But she could!

My Grandma
doesn't fly a helicopter
over the zoo...

But she could!

My Grandma
doesn't hang glide over
Golden Gate Park...

But she could!

My Grandma
doesn't catch home run
balls in a kayak...

But she could!

My Grandma
doesn't windsurf
to Alcatraz...

But she could!

My Grandma
doesn't sell crabs on
Fisherman's Wharf...

But she could!

My Grandma
doesn't do a groovy
dance to the music in
Haight-Ashbury...

But she could!

My Grandma
could do lots of things,
but I'm so happy with
the one thing she does
the best...

Parrot

Can you find these animals in the book?

Squirrel with flowers

Chocolate Moose

Seagull

Squirrel with bling

Sea Otter

Crab

Buffalo

Lion

Giraffe

Seal

Dolphin

Can you make these San Francisco Sounds?

 Have some fun and keep repeating until you drive someone crazy!

Sea lions at Pier 39
Arf-arf-arf! (Clap-clap-clap!)

Cable car on Powell Street
Ring-a-ding-ding!

A Union Square street musician drummer
Rat-a-tat-tat!

A duck in a pond
Quack-quack-quack!

A baby on a tour bus
Waaah-waaah-waaah!

Dolphins under the Golden Gate Bridge
Eeee-eeeee-eeeee!

A Market Street cookie truck
Beeep-beeeep-beeep-da-beep-beep-beep!

Monkeys at the zoo
Oo-oo-oo, eee-eee-eee!

A motorcycle in Haight Ashbury
Vroom-vroom-vroom-vroom-vroom-vroooooom!

A dog in Golden Gate Park
Ruff-ruff-ruff (take a breath) ruff-ruff-ruff!

Alcatraz Ferry horn
Arrrrrr-arrrrrrrr-arrrrrrr!

An airplane at the airport
Rrrroar-rrrroar-rrrroar!

A seagull in the Bay
At-at-at-at-at-at!

Share more laughs with these fun books!

**Available at
www.RicDilz.com**

Published by RICDesign, LLC, Boulder, Colorado

ISBN: 978-0-9859684-6-5

Library of Congress Control Number: 2015916855

Printed in China